The PINK HAT

by Andrew Joyner

Dragonfly Books New York

First there wasn't a hat.

Then . . .

there was.

It was a pink hat.

A cozy pink hat.

That is, until . . .

A cat grabbed the hat.

It was a fun hat.

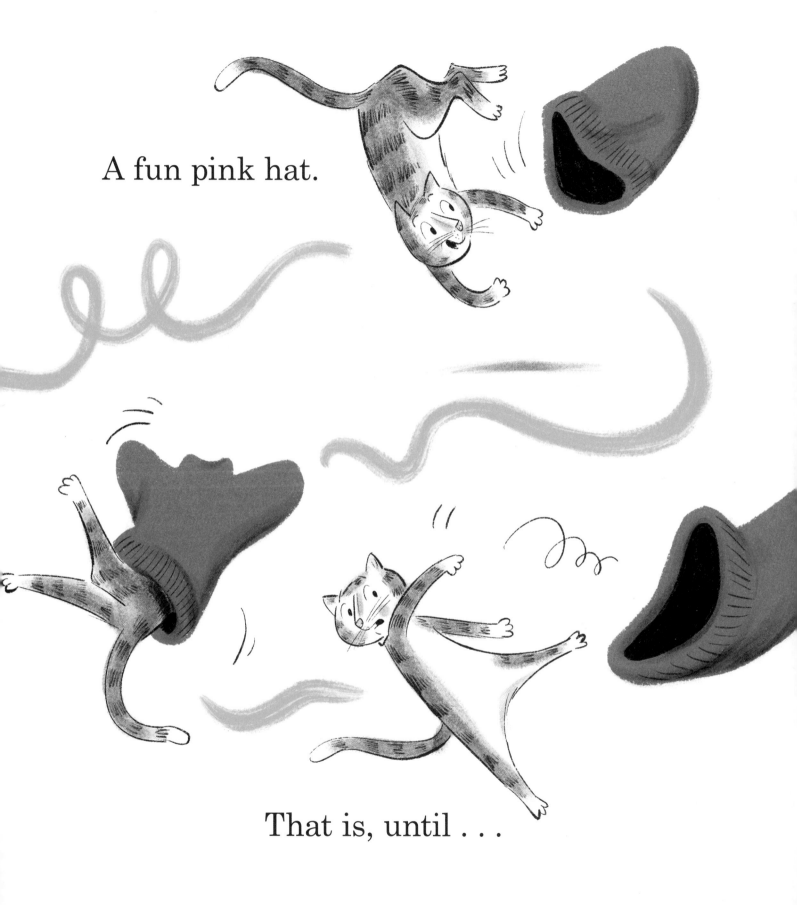

A fun pink hat.

That is, until . . .

Some children found the hat.

It was a
hard-to-reach hat.

A hard-to-reach
pink hat.

That is, until . . .

A baby caught the hat.

It was a warm hat.

A warm pink hat.

That is, until . . .

A dog swiped the hat.

It was a speedy hat.

A speedy pink hat.

That is, until . . .

A girl saved the hat.

And took it home.

The girl washed
the hat.

And dried the hat.

And wore the hat.

She wore it again.

And again.

And again.

That is, until . . .

She wore her pink hat,

and everyone else wore one, too!

On January 21, 2017, an estimated 5 million women, men, and children marched in 82 countries, on all 7 continents. The event was called the Women's March, and it was one of the largest political demonstrations in history. This joyous and peaceful protest united people and communities behind one simple message: women's rights are human rights.

For all the women who march us forward.
And for Kirsten, Lee, and Beck,
with love and gratitude.

Text and illustrations copyright © 2017 by Andrew Joyner
All rights reserved. Published in the United States by Dragonfly Books,
an imprint of Random House Children's Books,
a division of Penguin Random House LLC, New York.
Originally published in hardcover in the United States by Schwartz & Wade Books,
an imprint of Random House Children's Books, New York, in 2017.
Dragonfly Books with the colophon is a registered trademark of Penguin Random House LLC.
Visit us on the Web! rhcbooks.com
Educators and librarians, for a variety of teaching tools, visit us at RHTeachersLibrarians.com
Library of Congress Cataloging-in-Publication Data is available upon request.
ISBN 978-1-5247-7226-0 (trade) — ISBN 978-1-5247-7227-7 (lib. bdg.)
ISBN 978-1-5247-7228-4 (ebook) — ISBN 978-0-593-11896-2 (pbk.)
The text of this book is set in 24-point Century Schoolbook Pro.
The illustrations were rendered digitally in the Procreate app.
MANUFACTURED IN CHINA
10 9 8 7 6 5 4 3 2 1
First Dragonfly Books Edition 2019
Random House Children's Books supports the First Amendment and celebrates the right to read.